adapted by Rebecca McCarthy

based on the screenplays "Trading Day" written by Scott Kreamer
and "The Tell-Tale Toy" by Eric Horsted and Scott Kreamer

illustrated by Steve Lambe

Simon Spotlight/Nickelodeon

New York London Toronto Sydney New Delhi

designed by Victor Joseph Ochoa

Based on the TV series *Fanboy and Chum Chum*™ as seen on Nickelodeon™

SIMON SPOTLIGHT/NICKELODEON
An imprint of Simon & Schuster Children's Publishing Division 1230 Avenue of the Americas, New York, NY 10020. Copyright © 2012 Viacom International, Inc. All rights reserved. NICKELODEON, *Fanboy and Chum Chum,* and all related titles, logos, and characters are trademarks of Viacom International, Inc. All rights reserved, including the right of reproduction in whole or in part in any form. SIMON SPOTLIGHT and colophon are registered trademarks of Simon & Schuster, Inc. For information about special discounts for bulk purchases, please contact Simon & Schuster Special Sales at 1-866-506-1949 or business@simonandschuster.com.
Manufactured in the USA 1211 OFF
First Edition 10 9 8 7 6 5 4 3 2 1
ISBN 978-1-4424-2743-3 (pbk)
ISBN 978-1-4424-4686-1 (hc)

THE TELL-TALE TOY

What did the ocean say to Fanboy?

Nothing—it just waved!

CHAPTER ONE

Inside the Fanlair, the adventurous superfan of all things awesome, Fanboy, and his trusty sidekick, Chum Chum, peered eagerly through the two mail slots in the front door.

"When's that postman gonna get here?" groaned Fanboy impatiently. "Doesn't he know we want to play Junk-Mail-lympics?!"

Just then a handful of envelopes, pamphlets, and packages fell through the two mail slots into the baskets waiting below.

"Junk mail!" the boys shouted in delight, leaping into the air to give each other a high five.

Fanboy formally announced, "Let the games begin." He reached into his basket and pulled out a small bottle. "Trial-size dandruff shampoo," he said, challenging Chum Chum to come up with something even more unbelievably awesome.

"Oooh, a coupon for free ranch dressing!" Chum Chum uttered, waving the paper in Fanboy's face.

Fanboy reached into his basket again and shouted, "A sample-size tube of Sleeperhold Denture Cream!"

Chum Chum reached for the last piece of junk mail. "I got a cardboard box," he announced.

"I believe victory is mine," Fanboy stated proudly.

But then Chum Chum turned the box around and said, "A cardboard box

from . . . the Toyco Toy Company!"
Fanboy saw that inside the box was a
brand-new action figure!

"Whaaaaa?" he gasped.

"It's finally here!" Chum Chum shouted,
waving the box around.

"An Ultra-Ninja figure with Hi-Ya
Action Hand!" Fanboy cried. Completely
forgetting about the Junk-Mail-lympics,
Fanboy got down on his knees and
begged, "Let me see it! Let me see it!"

"Uh, sure," said Chum Chum warily, and he held the box a few feet away from Fanboy. "See?"

"No, no, no, no!" demanded Fanboy, bouncing up and down with excitement. "I mean *see* it. You know, with my hands? Gimmegimmegimmegimme!"

Chum Chum hesitated. "I don't know, Fanboy. Whenever you touch my toys, you always break them."

But Fanboy wasn't listening. His eyes were fixed on the Ultra-Ninja box, his body trembling with eagerness, his arms outstretched with stretchiness—he *needed* to play with that toy.

But Chum Chum was determined. "No, Fanboy. You're gonna break it."

Fanboy put on his best shocked expression. "How dare you, sir! Wherever would you get such an idea?"

Where? From reality.

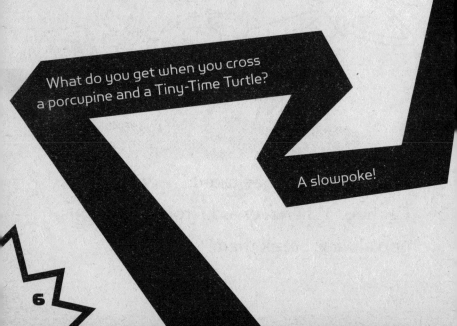

What do you get when you cross a porcupine and a Tiny-Time Turtle?

A slowpoke!

CHAPTER TWO

Chum Chum tried to explain. "You broke my teddy bear," he said. Indeed, Fanboy remembered the time he accidentally ripped the arm off of Chum Chum's new teddy bear.

Chum Chum pouted. "You broke my Man-Arctica plate," he moaned. Fanboy *did* remember when he accidentally broke the Man-Arctica plate while practicing his aim with his slingshot.

Chum Chum frowned. "You broke my Tiny-Time Turtle." Fanboy confessed that, yes, he had burned Tiny-Time Turtle with a blowtorch . . . accidentally, of course.

"Wow, you're right," Fanboy admitted. "I do break all your stuff. I'm sorry, Chum Chum. I feel awful."

This was all Chum Chum needed to hear. "It's okay, Fanboy. It's just who you are. And I accept that about you."

"Okay, Chum Chum. I promise I will not touch it," Fanboy stated.

"Really?"

"Let's shake on it . . . with the Fanboy–

Chum Chum Super-Shake of Trust!" Fanboy sang as he grabbed Chum Chum's hand. Chum Chum grabbed Fanboy's other hand, and they wiggled their fingers and leaped into the air. A couple more hand slaps and a hip bump sealed the deal. Not only had Fanboy given Chum Chum his word, he had also given him . . . a broken arm!

It was an accident, of course. On coming down from their midair super-shake, Fanboy had landed on Chum Chum's arm. Chum Chum wasn't angry though. As always, he happily forgave his friend.

"Well, I think I'm going to run down to the hospital and get my arm bone set," said Chum Chum cheerfully. "They gave me this card that said the tenth cast is free." He made it to the door, and Fanboy opened it for him. But as he walked out,

Fanboy accidentally shut the door too soon—right on Chum Chum's broken arm! Ouch!

But Chum Chum wasn't fazed. "See ya later, Fanboy!" he chirped as he headed down to the hospital.

Fanboy was left alone in the Fanlair . . . alone with Ultra-Ninja!

Top Four Reasons the Ultra-Ninja is the Greatest Action Figure of All Time (according to the Toyco Toy Company):

1. Ready for action, right out of the box!

2. Once you own one, you can fight the evil forces of . . . other Ultra-Ninja figures! Collect them all!

3. Hi-Ya Action Hand, the ultimate hand of action.

4. Now available: Ultra-Ninjette, Ultra-Baby-Ninja, Ultra-Ninja-Dog—all sold separately.

CHAPTER THREE

Fanboy almost called out after his friend, "Chum Chum! You forgot your Ultra-Ninja! I'll bring it to you." But then he caught himself. "Oh, wait. Can't touch it," he said. So instead he called out, "Uhh . . . don't worry, it'll be safe here with me!" Fanboy closed the door. He was determined to keep his promise, but boy, did he want to play with that toy. . . .

"Control yourself, Fanboy!" he said.

You owe it to Chum Chum. Just don't look at it!" But Fanboy did look at it. He *had* to look at it. It begged to be looked at. But looking was fine. He just couldn't *touch* it . . . even though it also begged to be touched.

"Must resist!" Fanboy reminded himself. "Must get away!" But no matter how hard he tried to forget about the toy, he could not stay away from it. It was as tempting and forbidden as a shiny new drum set in the middle of a library.

"I'm weak! I admit it, I'm weak," Fanboy moaned. "Chum Chum wouldn't care if I grazed it a little. I mean, all he said was, 'Don't touch it.' He didn't say 'Don't touch it, don't touch it.' Two totally different things, right?"

But even his conscience didn't agree with him. "What am I doing? Chum Chum's my best friend. We even did the Super-Shake of Trust—the world's most trusted super-shake!" Fanboy's voice was full of conviction, but his eyes kept floating back toward Ultra-Ninja. His feet started moving him closer to it, like a zombie in search of brains. Fanboy resisted with all his might. "I shall not—nay—I *will* not betray my Chum Chum!"

But then suddenly he looked down and found Ultra-Ninja resting in his hands! How did that happen?

"No. No-no-no. Back you go. Into your box," he said frantically. But as he looked at the toy, he couldn't help noticing how awesome it was. How new. How . . . action-y.

"Feel that fresh factory plastic," Fanboy said. "And look at that high-gloss finish. And let's not forget the superawesome, often-imitated-but-never-duplicated Hi-Ya Action Hand!" Fanboy enthusiastically pressed the button on the back of the toy and shouted, "Hi-ya! Hi-ya! Hi-ya!"

But the toy did not move.

Hey, where's the Hi-Ya action? Fanboy wondered. He paced back and forth. Suddenly he stopped and thought, *Wait a minute, this must be a test to teach me an important lesson . . . ALWAYS PRESS HARDER!* Fanboy slammed his finger on the button a hundred times and then jumped on it a hundred more until . . . crunch!

The toy broke into pieces—many, many pieces.

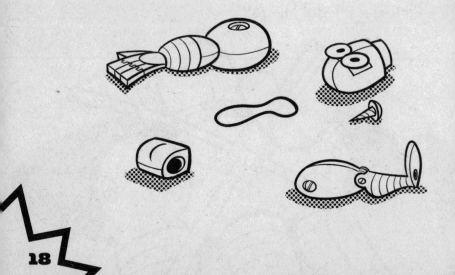

CHAPTER FOUR

broke it!" cried Fanboy. "Chum Chum's going to be so disappointed in me!" He panicked and jumped wildly like a kangaroo on a pogo stick until, finally, he fainted.

After a few moments Fanboy recovered and stood up. Then he looked down, saw the broken toy, and fainted again. A minute later Fanboy recovered and stood up. Once again he saw the broken toy, shouted, "What have I done?", and fainted. Fanboy continued to recover and faint as the sun set and the moon rose in the sky.

The next morning Fanboy woke up with the brilliant idea to perform emergency surgery on Ultra-Ninja. "I can rebuild him," he declared seriously. "I have the technology."

Wearing a surgeon's mask and scrubs, and assisted by a seagull who just happened to be standing by in the Fanlair, Fanboy began the operation.

"Scalpel," he requested.

"Tweezers," he requested.

"Hot glue gun," he continued.

"Screwdriver," he commanded. A few twists, turns, staples, and snaps, and it was done.

"It's perfect!" Fanboy exclaimed loudly. Indeed, the toy was fixed . . .

until the seagull sneezed, and it burst
into pieces again. Fanboy gasped and
launched himself into a renewed state of
frenzy.

At last he decided he had no choice now but to hide the evidence. Chum Chum would be home any minute and he had to act fast. But where could he hide all the plastic pieces?

"Come on, Fanboy, use your head," he said to himself. "Use your head, use your head." Then he snapped his fingers and realized he had come up with the perfect hiding place—in his head! Fanboy lifted the flap on top of his head, spilled the pieces inside, and flopped, satisfied, on the couch. "Fanboy, you are a genius," he said, closing his eyes and grinning.

"Fanboy! Fanboy!" bellowed a thunderous voice, causing Fanboy to stir and sit up.

"Whoa! What's going on?" Fanboy asked.

Suddenly the roof of the entire Fanlair was lifted up. Fanboy opened his eyes and saw . . . a giant Chum Chum!

"You broke my toy!" scolded Giant Chum Chum. Fanboy recoiled in horror as Giant Chum Chum reached down to grab him!

Suddenly Fanboy woke up shaking. What a nightmare! He hadn't felt that scared since the time the cafeteria ran out of Tater Tots!

Fanboy coughed up all the pieces of Ultra-Ninja and spit them out onto the floor. "Whoa, that toy did not agree with me," he decided. He had to find a new hiding place. Quickly he swept the pieces under the rug. It looked a little lumpy, but it worked. Kind of.

"Perfect," he said, clapping his hands. "Now I just have to think of what I'm going to tell Chum Chum."

"Tell me what?" Fanboy heard a voice say behind him. Startled, he turned and saw that Chum Chum had returned from the hospital and was standing in the doorway!

The advantages and disadvantages of underwear:... Discuss.

CHAPTER FIVE

Aaaahh!" Fanboy panicked. "I mean . . . I was going to tell you that . . . you're the best pal in the world, buddy, old pal!"

"Aww, thanks," Chum Chum said affectionately. Then he looked down at the rug and asked, "Hey, is our rug lumpier than usual?"

"N-nope. Don't think so," stammered Fanboy. He grabbed Chum Chum by his unbroken arm and steered him away from the lumpy rug, sweeping him up the stairs. He talked frantically, trying to make Chum Chum think about other things.

"Hey, b-best friend of mine," he sputtered, "why don't we take the long way around and spend some time together? You know, get some exercise. Get the old ticker tocking. Mmm, smell that fresh recirculated air."

Chum Chum just stared at his friend curiously as they walked up the ramp to the loft. He had the feeling that something wasn't quite right. "Fanboy, are you okay?" Chum Chum asked.

"Sure I am," Fanboy insisted as they went down the loft's slide. "Why wouldn't I be? Never felt better in all my—" Just then they landed on the couch, right in front of the rug!

"Aaaaahh!" Fanboy screamed again.

Now Chum Chum *knew* something was wrong, and Fanboy knew there was no more hiding it. It was time to tell the truth.

Fanboy exhaled deeply and cried, "I'm so sorry, Chum Chum!" He wailed and fell to his knees. "I didn't listen. I didn't honor the Super-Shake of Trust! I broke your Ultra-Ninja!"

"My . . . Ultra-Ninja?" Chum Chum said slowly. Fanboy nodded wretchedly. He couldn't even look his friend in the eye.

"Is the box okay?" Chum Chum demanded.

"What?" Fanboy asked, confused.

"The box, man! Where's the box?" Chum Chum shouted anxiously.

"Uh, it's over there." Fanboy pointed to the empty box up against the wall.

Chum Chum ran over and hugged it with a big sigh of relief. "Oh, it's okay! Thank goodness!" he crooned.

Fanboy wondered why Chum Chum wasn't angry with him. He did, after all, break the new toy.

"Oh," Chum Chum explained, "I was going to give the toy to you anyway. I only wanted the box." Then Chum Chum put the box on his head and started playing tugboat captain. Shuffling back and forth, he tooted, "Chumma-chumma-chumma, choo-choo!"

Fanboy couldn't believe his eyes. As Chum Chum shuffled by, pulling his imaginary tugboat whistle, Fanboy started to faint once again. On his way down, he considered how lucky he was to have such a forgiving best friend.

"That boy sure is easy to please," he noted as everything faded to black.

THE eND

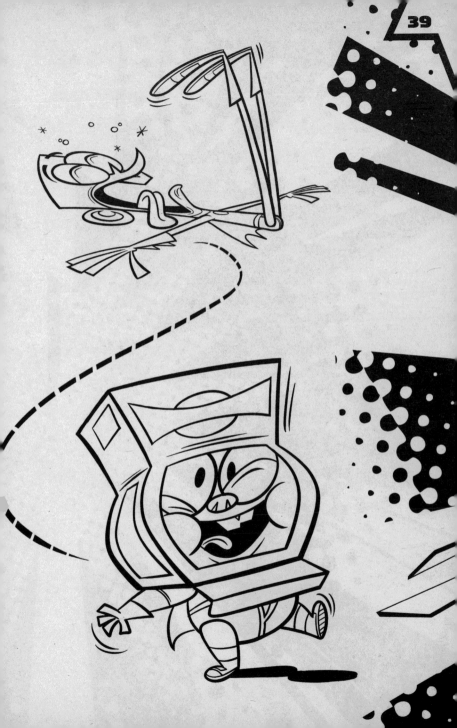

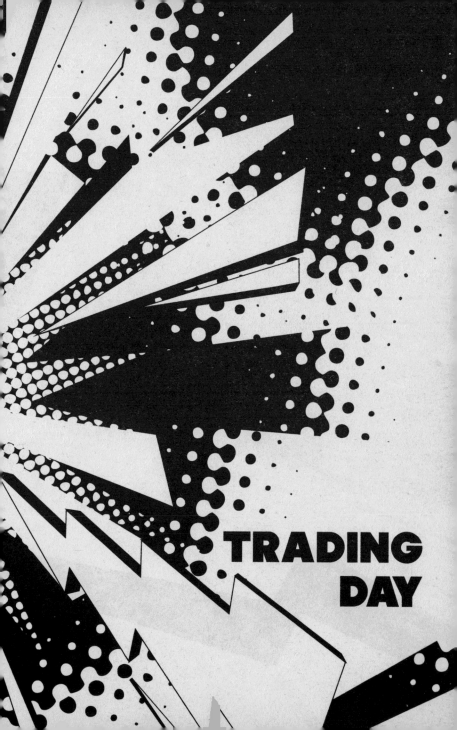

TRADING
DAY

CHAPTER ONE

ow many times do I have to tell you? Chum Chum is *not* a toy!" Fanboy shouted as he zipped around Oz Comix, holding Chum Chum up over his head with one hand. Yo, one of Fanboy and Chum Chum's classmates, giggled as she chased after Chum Chum, jumping up in the air in an effort to reach him.

"I know," said Yo. She giggled and wiggled as she tried to keep herself

under control. "But he's just so cute and . . . Chum Chum-y! I just want to clip him to my belt and take him wherever I go."

Suddenly, faster than Fanboy could blink, Yo snatched Chum Chum and *did* clip him to her belt! *How'd she do that so fast?* Fanboy wondered. You had to wake up pretty early in the morning to stay ahead of Yo. With a frustrated snort, Fanboy snatched Chum Chum back.

"¡Silencio!" ordered Oz, who stood at the counter, his eyes fixed on the television as if they were glued to the screen. "You can talk during the cartoons, but *this* is a *commercial*." Fanboy, Chum Chum, and Yo skidded to a halt in front of the TV.

On the screen they saw a boy and a girl sitting with their toys, looking totally bored. Suddenly a gigantic robot crashed through the ceiling, destroying their house! "It's Mecha-Tech! Mecha-Tech! Mecha-Tech!" howled the TV announcer. "The toy robot that does whatever *you* want it to do!"

"I await your command!" said the toy.

"Mecha-Tech, bake me a cupcake!" said the girl. The robot opened the door to his chest and *BAM!* He pulled out a fresh-baked cupcake with pink frosting!

"Mecha-Tech, do a slam dunk!" said the boy.

The robot grabbed the boy, rolled him up into a ball, dribbled him, and slam-dunked him into the toy basketball net hanging on the bedroom door!

The TV announcer repeated, "Mecha-Tech! Mecha-Tech! Mecha-Tech! He's yours to command so you can have fun! Fun! FUN!"

Fanboy's eyes widened as he dreamed of all the amazing things he could command Mecha-Tech to do. Like fetch him a jar of mayonnaise! Or drag itself around on the floor!

Or even scrape the burnt parts off his toast! Fanboy drooled at the thought of a toy that could do all these stupendous things! He knew he just had to have one.

When Oz clicked off the television, Fanboy snapped back to reality. He noticed Yo trying to slink out of the store, with her mouth full of . . . something. He did a double take and then realized Chum Chum was missing! He leaped over to the door like a wild spider monkey to intercept Yo.

"Going somewhere, Yo?" he demanded. Yo shrugged innocently, but Fanboy could hear Chum Chum mumbling inside. "Okay," Fanboy said, "cough him up."

With a loud belch, Yo spat out a saliva-covered Chum Chum. Yep, Fanboy would have to wake up pretty early in the morning to stay ahead of Yo. . . .

Mecha-Tech awaits your command! What would you have Mecha-Tech do?

CHAPTER TWO

The next day at school, Fanboy stood at his locker, swooning over a picture of a Mecha-Tech robot he had mounted in a very expensive, solid-gold picture frame. "Oh Mecha-Tech," he said, sighing, "why can't you be mine?"

Chum Chum popped out of the locker next to him. "Because you spent all your money on that picture frame?"

"Gah, what am I going to do without a Mecha-Tech of my very own?" Fanboy

moaned. "Fetch my own mayonnaise?"

"Don't worry, Fanboy, you'll think of something," Chum Chum said confidently.

When Fanboy and Chum Chum walked into their classroom, what they saw made their eyes pop out of their heads and their jaws drop to the floor.

Every kid had a Mecha-Tech! One girl cradled hers like a baby. One boy was having a burp contest with his. Their fellow student, the wizard Kyle, leafed through a *Preteen Wizard* magazine while his Mecha-Tech made him a hot, frothy latte. Even their teacher Mr. Mufflin had his own Mecha-Tech! The room echoed with the sound of happy people playing with their new Mecha-Tech robots. Fanboy gazed upon the room as if he was standing at the edge of an Olympic-size swimming pool full of Frosty Freeze without a straw.

Yo dangled her Mecha-Tech inches from Fanboy's face and taunted, "Hey, Fanboy, where's your Mecha-Tech? Aww, didn't you get one?"

Fanboy went dizzy and his mouth was

dry. "No . . . have . . . money. . . ." was all he managed to say.

"Aww, pity," Yo said smugly. Then she thought for a moment and said, "I'll trade you mine."

Fanboy's eyes lit up. He jumped around Yo like a terrier who could smell doggie treats in his owner's pocket. "Really?!?

What do you want? I will give you anything! Name your price!" he begged.

Just then Chum Chum came over
wearing a trash can on his head. "Look,
Fanboy! I'm a Mecha-Tech. I ate your
commando! Chumma-chumma-chumma."

As Chum Chum repeatedly bashed his
head into the wall, Yo giggled adoringly
and gave Fanboy a look. In a flash Fanboy
realized what she had in mind. He gasped
in horror.

"You don't actually think that I would trade you Chum Chum?" he huffed.

"C'mon," Yo said reassuringly. "I'll take real good care of him, just like I do with all my digital pets. Just for one day? Please?"

"I don't know. . . ." Fanboy hesitated.

Yo held her Mecha-Tech up to Fanboy's face again. "I am ready to fetch you a jar of mayonnaise," the robot announced.

The temptation was too much. It was

torture, like being at the edge of a freshly polished wood floor in cotton socks and being told not to run and slide on it. Fanboy just had to have it!

He turned to Yo. She had an eager look on her face. As Fanboy extended his hand to make the deal, she relaxed into a satisfied grin.

Later, on the playground, Chum Chum couldn't wait to play with Fanboy. Fanboy struggled to come up with an excuse for why he would not be there.

He gently explained, "Well, Chum Chum, today, you're going to play with Yo. I can't play with you because, well, they just sent a monkey in a diaper into outer space, and I need to go up there to change it."

"Why can't I come?" Chum Chum asked.

"He's been in the same diaper for three weeks. I'm just trying to spare you, buddy," Fanboy explained.

"You always look out for me," Chum Chum said and smiled warmly. "But still, outer space can be dangerous. You might need my help."

"Oh no, that's okay," Fanboy said. "I can handle danger. Remember the time I hiked Great Frosty Mountain?"

"Yeah, we did that together," Chum Chum said.

"Right," Fanboy agreed. "Um . . . well, remember the time I rode the Bathtub of Fury down the Stairway of Doom?"

"We did that together too," Chum Chum reminded him, scraping his shoe back and forth along the sand.

"Oh yeah. Well, remember that time I went swimming right after I ate?"

"Yeah. You were on your own there."

"See? I can handle danger by myself!"

"Huh. Okay, have a good time, Fanboy!" said Chum Chum. He hugged his friend good-bye and ran off to play. Fanboy got a little teary eyed. Leaving Chum Chum was more difficult for him than playing the No Talking game after drinking seven Frosty Freezes, but he reminded himself that it was just for one day.

What does a Mecha-Tech baby drink out of?

A robottle.

CHAPTER THREE

Fanboy said to Yo, all business, "Remember, this is a *borrow*, not a *trade*."

She nodded and promised, "And then we trade back."

Reassured, Fanboy walked off with Yo's Mecha-Tech, leaving Chum Chum behind.

He skipped with the robot to the picnic tables at one end of the playground. "I await your command!" said Mecha-Tech.

So many commands popped into Fanboy's head. *Make me a new super-suit! Fly me to Aruba! Build me the ultimate snow fort! Peel all the white stringy things off my orange! Find me a map to a pirate's treasure! Take me kayaking in the fjords of Norway!* Fanboy's head spun with excitement. Which command should he choose? Finally, he blurted out the best one of all: "Mecha-Tech, I command you to dance."

Mecha-Tech began to break-dance on the bench of the picnic table. Fanboy lay on the bench and smiled in wonder as he watched his new toy go.

"Mecha-Tech, you are a little superstar," he said. "Am I right, Chum Chum?" But then Fanboy remembered Chum Chum was not there; Fanboy was alone.

"Well, I'm sure he's having fun," Fanboy consoled himself. "It's good for him to get out and hang with new people. *But* I guess it wouldn't hurt to peek in and see how he's doing." Fanboy ordered Mecha-Tech to give him a pair of binoculars, and then he looked through them to find Chum Chum and Yo.

On the far end of the playground, he could see Yo riding Chum Chum like a horse and laughing. Fanboy sighed. "Flying pony was *our* game," he said a little wistfully.

Fanboy was interrupted by the mechanical voice of Mecha-Tech.

"I await your command!" said the toy.

Fanboy turned away from the binoculars, noticed the robot, and said glumly, "Hmm? Oh yeah, you."

Meanwhile Yo rode Chum Chum like a pony out of the playground and into a clearing. They came upon a giant glass dome, with a little doghouse inside. There was also a tall ladder leaning against the side that led to an opened hatch up top.

Yo opened her eyes wide. "Someone—not me—left this here! What luck for us!"

"Wow, that *is* lucky," agreed Chum Chum. "I wonder what kind of humongous digital pet lives in there."

Yo rubbed her hands together. "I don't know," she said, her eyes wider than ever. "Why don't you follow that trail of chocolate-covered raisins up that ladder and find out?"

Chum Chum wasn't one to resist chocolate-covered raisins. Eagerly he climbed the ladder. When he got to the top hatch, Yo tossed one more raisin into the giant dome. Chum Chum leaped in after it. Once inside, he called out, "Hello? Anybody home?"

Suddenly Yo closed the hatch behind him. "There is now," she chortled. She took the ladder away and clapped her hands together delightedly. *Chum Chum* was her new digital pet.

Write a song about Chum Chum that includes the word "chum-tastic." Then sing it in your loudest possible voice!

CHAPTER FOUR

Back at school Fanboy sat on the front steps, staring sadly at a photo of him and Chum Chum. Mecha-Tech zoomed over, using his rocket feet, holding a moon rock that he had gotten from the moon itself, but Fanboy didn't seem to care.

"Whatever. Just put it with the other stuff," he said. Mecha-Tech tossed the moon rock onto a pile that contained an ice-cream cart, a Frosty Freeze machine,

and a TV. Fanboy looked at it all, shrugged, and sighed. "Meh." Playing without Chum Chum was turning out to be as boring as sitting in detention watching his teacher, Mr. Mufflin, eat a baloney sandwich.

"I await your command!" said Mecha-Tech.

"You know what?" Fanboy said, resolved. "There's only one thing you *can* do for me. You can be like Chum Chum! And if you can't do that, I don't want you."

"What is a Chum Chum?" said Mecha-Tech, searching his data banks.

"What is a Chum Chum?" Fanboy repeated. He stood and tried to explain. "He's a snow day when you've got a spelling test. He's the marshmallows in hot chocolate and the sludge that forms on the bottom. He's a pudding fight that spills into a French-fry battle and escalates into a fish-stick war!" Then he broke down and sobbed, "Oh, what have I done? I want my Chum Chum back!"

"I await your command!" said Mecha-Tech.

Fanboy sneered, "Is that all you can say? Argh! That's it! I'm trading you back right now!" But then when Fanboy went to pick him up, the toy's arm broke off!

"Uh-oh," said Fanboy. Instantly Mecha-Tech sounded a piercing distress alarm, which caused Fanboy to drop him and cover his ears.

"Mecha-Tech under attack! Calling Mecha-Tech defense squad!" With that, Mecha-Tech alerted all the other Mecha-Techs at school to his "unarmed" situation.

One by one, they responded, forming a toy-robot army! And this army had one goal—to destroy Fanboy.

Meanwhile, back in the clearing, Yo pushed three control buttons, which made Chum Chum do backflips

Where do boobleberries grow, anyway?

for boobleberries. Or was he flipping because he just really liked boobleberries? With Chum Chum it was hard to know for sure. Suddenly Yo heard Fanboy's scream and the sound of Mecha-Tech lasers being fired. She smiled as if she had expected this to happen all along. Then she initiated the second phase of her master plan. She pushed the control button that forced Chum Chum to take a nap. He marched like a zombie into the little doghouse, and fell asleep instantly. All that was left for Yo to do was wait.

Back at the playground Fanboy dodged lasers left and right until the Mecha-Techs had him surrounded.

"Surrender!" Yo's Mecha-Tech ordered.

But "surrender" was not in Fanboy's vocabulary. Literally.

"Time to put away the toys!"
he cried. And then he charged! Fanboy
used his superfan skills to beat, karate-
chop, and slash the Mecha-Tech army to
bits! He even threw in some action-hero
catchphrases for emphasis.

"Some *disassembly* required!" *Crash!*

"Pain sold separately!" *Splat!*

Who would win in a Battle of the Toys—Mecha-Tech or Ultra-Ninja? Discuss. Use examples from the text to support your theory.

Fanboy flipped and tumbled over the enemy like underpants in the dryer, and at the end of the cycle, he emerged victorious!

And now, what he wanted more than anything in the world was to go get his best friend back. . . .

CHAPTER FIVE

An exhausted Fanboy arrived at the giant dome and knocked on the glass. Yo poked her head out. "Oh, hello, Fanboy," she said evenly. "What brings you here?"

"Yo," he said, "I want my Chum Chum. It's time to trade back."

Yo grinned and tumbled out. She noticed the mangled robot in Fanboy's hand and exclaimed, "What happened to my Mecha-Tech?" The only part left of the toy was its head, which said weakly, "I ate your commando." Then it exploded.

"Ummmm . . ." said Fanboy. "Got any . . . tape?"

Seeing the toy completely destroyed, Yo's grin widened into a triumphant smile. She squealed happily, "You don't have anything to trade back!"

Fanboy grunted, confused.

"That means Chum Chum's mine!" She clapped gleefully.

Suddenly Fanboy realized that Yo had the entire master plan worked out from the beginning. She knew that Fanboy would break her toy. How? Because Fanboy broke all his toys, and all his friends' toys too. In fact Fanboy never met a toy he didn't break. Yo traded him her brand-new toy, knowing that Fanboy would break it and not be able to trade back for Chum Chum at the end of the day. It was genius. And there was nothing Fanboy or Chum Chum could do to change things.

"A deal is a deal," Yo said triumphantly.

Fanboy didn't know what to say. He looked helplessly at the giant dome.

Just then Chum Chum rolled out of the doghouse and woke up.

"Wha?" he said, wiping the sweat from his brow. "How long was I out? Fanboy, what's going on?"

Fanboy looked upon his loyal friend. Chum Chum's hair glistened in the sunlight, like a nose hair after a sneeze. Fanboy then confessed sadly, "I'm sorry, Chum Chum.

I lied to you. I traded you to Yo so I could play with her Mecha-Tech, and now you're stuck in there forever!"

Chum Chum pouted. "You're a bad friend," he said. Fanboy lowered his head. But then Chum Chum added, "But I'm going to miss you."

It was more than Fanboy could handle. He envisioned himself alone for the rest of his days—just one sad couch potato on the gravy boat of life. And gravy boats were meant for two!

"Please, Yo!" he begged. "I can't live

without my Chum Chum! There must be some way to work this out!"

A rascally look crept across Yo's face. "Maybe there is. . . ." she admitted.

For the rest of the day, Fanboy and Chum Chum did backflips for boobleberries in Yo's giant dome. They were her pets, but they were together, and that was more important to Fanboy than all the toys in the world.

THE END